Twelfth Night

About the Author

Beverley Birch grew up in Kenya and first came to England,
where she now lives with her husband and
two daughters, at the age of fifteen. After completing
an MA in Economics and Sociology, Beverley became
an editor at Penguin. Within a few weeks she was offered the
chance to work on children's books and has been involved in
children's publishing – as both editor and writer – ever since.

She has had over forty books published, from picture books
and novels to science biographies and retellings of classic
works. All her titles have received critical acclaim and her work
has been translated into more than a dozen languages. Her
latest novel for teenagers, *Rift*, was published in 2006.

Shakespeare's Tales

Twelfth Night

Retold by Beverley Birch

Illustrated by Jenny Williams

WAYLAND

For my mother, with love

Text copyright © 1988 Beverley Birch
Illustrations copyright © 2006 Jenny Williams
First published in *Shakespeare's Stories: Comedies* in 1988 by
Macdonald & Co (Publishers) Limited.
This edition first published in 2006 by
Wayland, an imprint of Hachette Children's Books

The right of Beverley Birch to be identified as author
and Jenny Williams as the illustrator of this Work has
been asserted by them in accordance with the
Copyright, Designs and Patents Act 1988.

Cover and text design: Rosamund Saunders

Hachette Children's Books
338 Euston Road, London NW1 3BH

Printed and bound in the United Kingdom

ISBN-10: 0 7502 4964 1
ISBN-13: 978 0 7502 4964 5

The Cast

Duke Orsino – ruler of Illyria

Lady Olivia – a countess

Sir Toby Belch – a relative of Olivia

Sir Andrew Aguecheek – Sir Toby's companion

Feste – Olivia's court jester

Maria – Olivia's maid

Malvolio – Olivia's steward

Fabian – Olivia's servant

Viola

Cesario – Viola in disguise

Sebastian – Viola's twin brother

Antonio – Sebastian's friend

A sea captain

Duke Orsino was in love. Love perfumed the air with flowers, coloured the hills and cliffs with rosy light, filled the rooms in which Orsino roamed with wistful songs, their lilting notes drifting from palace balconies into the summer air.

'If music be the food of love, play on; give me excess of it,' he murmured to the strains of mournful melodies. He listened to a dying fall of notes. 'Oh, it came over my ear like the sweet sound that breathes upon a bank of violets ... '

The duke lived for love, and dreamed of love, and sighed for love's melancholy. Indeed, if Duke Orsino's servants were to admit it (which they would not), the duke was truly in love with love itself, though he believed that the object of his adoration was a youthful and most beautiful countess named Lady Olivia.

Unfortunately for Duke Orsino, Lady Olivia did not love him. She would not love him; she could not love him; this was her only answer to his proffered love. She could love no man, for she had vowed to mourn her brother's death behind a veil, shedding tears for him in seven long years of sorrow. Since her brother's death she had allowed no visitors, no company of men near her, nor would she until the end of mourning.

And so Duke Orsino languished for love of Lady Olivia, and Lady Olivia languished for love of her dead brother, until one day, there came a stranger to that prosperous land of fair Illyria ... Wild winds and towering waves off Illyria's rocky coast had plucked a passing ship and tossed it like a toy, spilling its passengers into the foaming waves to drift like flotsam and jetsam towards the shore.

As the storm had calmed, it threw them on the rocks, battered, drenched and exhausted by their battle with the sea, but nonetheless alive. But this was little comfort for the stranger, a young girl named Viola. Somewhere in that storm-tossed sea her twin brother, Sebastian had also been fighting for his life, and Sebastian was dearer to her than any other person in the world.

Was he dead? Or was it possible that he survived as she had? She begged the good sea captain flung ashore with her: could Sebastian be alive? The captain gave her hope: after their ship had splintered he had seen Sebastian bind himself to a mast still floating on the sea, and there he was when last the captain saw him.

'For saying so, there's gold!' Viola cried, her eyes alight with renewed hope.

But now she shivered, though the winds had softened and the air was growing warm again. What was she to do now? Here was a country she did not know, and she a woman, quite alone in it …

The captain saw how the young girl's fears were growing again and tried to calm them. This Illyria was a prosperous, friendly, pleasant land. He knew it well, for he had been born and bred not three hours travel from this very place. And it was ruled well by a most noble, gentle duke, Orsino.

'Orsino!' Viola said. 'I have heard my father speak of him. He was unmarried then.'

And so was he now, the captain said, though

there was talk among the people that he sought the love of the lady Olivia, who mourned her brother's recent death.

Already Viola had seen a possible escape from her predicament, for though her mind was much clouded with fears for her brother's life, she had quick wits and buoyant spirits to give her strength … She would have liked most to serve Olivia, for it seemed that this lady might be a partner in mourning a dead brother. But the sea captain was certain she would not be accepted as a servant at Olivia's house. Olivia admitted no one.

Yet might it not be possible to obtain a position at Duke Orsino's court? Quickly she enlisted the kindly captain's help: he must lend her clothes to disguise herself as a man. She would present herself as a page at the palace of Duke Orsino of Illyria!

'I'll serve this duke!' declared Viola. 'I can sing and speak to him in many sorts of music … ' enthusiasm for this plan began to revive her spirits and she set off with the captain, happy to have some purpose to lift her thoughts from the persistent terrors for her brother's life.

Was he dead? The thought rose again. She pushed it back. On, on, to her disguise … She would become Duke Orsino's page, and trust to time and hope. Only this good sea captain would know her true identity …

Viola's plan worked better than her wildest dreams. The grace and delicacy of her woman's shape was hidden beneath the clothes of a young man, her long fair hair tight-curled beneath a cap; and so this pretty girl was transformed into a handsome youth whose smooth, unbearded face and light voice only made the Duke Orsino think that his new page was young, not yet having reached the age of manhood. Viola, who in her page's disguise called herself Cesario, endeared herself to the love-sick duke with quite remarkable speed. The duke was quick to find that the 'young man' had an attentive ear and understanding eye. Within three days, 'Cesario' had heard the full history of Orsino's love for Olivia: each sigh, each loving message, each miserable rejection had been catalogued by the unhappy duke for his young page, as had the beauty, wisdom and glory of the object of his adoration, the fair Olivia.

Now Orsino asked Cesario to take up his pleas with Olivia, to be his tongue to her, and carry his messages of love.

Viola listened to the tale with a heart throbbing with more than sympathy. She watched the duke's agony of unrequited love as though it was her own. Indeed, it almost could have been, for beneath her boy's clothes, Viola, Orsino's faithful page 'Cesario', was herself suffering the pangs of unrequited love. Within three days, Viola had fallen fathoms deep in love with Duke Orsino!

And now the agony grew worse. Orsino was asking her to carry his love messages to Olivia who scorned his love – the love that she, Viola would give anything to possess! Well, she would take his messages, because of her own loyalty to the duke and (though she scarce admitted it) also because she was a little curious to find out more about Olivia.

Sir Toby Belch was as full of wind and good cheer as was his name. He was a large, rotund, jovial sort of man whose only aim in life was to consume as much food and drink as his enormous bulk could hold (preferably food and drink that others had paid for); and to do so with as much rollicking good fun, songs, games, and the exchange of wit as could be crammed into the time between getting up (recovering from being drunk), and going to bed, drunk and sated with good food.

Not content merely with his own carousing to disturb the gloom of mourning in Olivia's house, Sir Toby had seen fit to introduce another: one Sir Andrew Aguecheek, a gentleman as long and thin and pale as Sir Toby was round and plump and red. Nevertheless Sir Andrew was an excellent companion for Sir Toby, for though his brain was on the meagre side, his purse was deliciously robust and fat. More to the point, his purse was at the disposal of Sir Toby.

Sir Toby had devised a plan to keep himself in

drink and food for as long as he had appetite to consume them and the strength to open his mouth. Olivia was to be persuaded to marry Sir Andrew Aguecheek. This being the general line of strategy, for the moment the tactics required that the long, thin knight should hang about the house with Sir Toby on the chance of seeing Olivia. The more Sir Andrew hung about, the more time he had to while away; the more time he had to while away, the more money he must spend; the more money he spent, the more Sir Toby made himself jovially available to share it, to keep the hopeful suitor's spirits up, to exchange a song, a dance, a joke with him … and generally while away the days, weeks or months … as chance would have it.

For a place of sombre mourning, Olivia's house indeed contained a motley collection of souls: besides the undaunted Sir Toby and the aging Andrew Aguecheek, there was also Feste, Olivia's court jester, who had a tendency to wander off on business of his own whenever the fancy took

14

him, and who therefore also felt the sting of maid Maria's warning tongue.

'My lady will hang you for your absence!' she chided him. 'Make your excuses wisely …!'

And indeed, when Olivia entered, dressed head to foot in dark colours, accompanied by the sombre shadow of her steward, Malvolio, her face solemnly composed in that grieving look it had worn since her brother died, she was angry, seeing Feste.

'Take the Fool away,' she said, with a dismissive toss of her elegant head.

The Fool had quickly shaken out his wits and got them ready for fooling. He pulled his face into a mockery of her solemnity and mimicked that tossing head.

'Do you hear, fellows? Take away the lady,' he declared.

'Sir,' protested Olivia, her solemn face giving way to the temptation of a smile despite herself, 'I told them to take *you* away.'

'Give me leave,' said the Fool, catching that fleeting glimmer of mirth and determined to prise it

15

out so that his misdemeanours would be quite forgotten by Olivia, 'Give me leave to prove *you* a fool.'

'Can you do it?' asked Olivia, curious, for she had most decidedly foresworn all merriment.

'Good madonna, why do you mourn?' enquired the Fool, with mock solemnity.

'Good Fool, for my brother's death,' said Olivia, irritated to be so unfeelingly reminded of her grief.

'I think his soul is in hell, madonna,' announced the Fool.

'I know his soul is in heaven, Fool,' retorted Olivia.

'The more fool you, madonna, to mourn for your brother's soul being in heaven. Take away the fool!'

Despite her determination not to, Olivia laughed. She turned to Malvolio, 'What do you think of this Fool, Malvolio? Does he not improve?'

Malvolio, it must be said, disapproved. What, precisely, it was that Malvolio disapproved of, would be difficult to say, for Malvolio's sharp nose was tilted in the air at everything and everyone he saw, his nostrils flared as though a most unpleasant smell was caught beneath them, his lips pressed hard together with an air of pained endurance, and his eyes half-closed as though it were pure agony to waste their light on mortals such as these …

'I marvel your ladyship takes delight in such a barren rascal,' he intoned with a disdainful look towards Feste. 'I saw him put down the other day with an ordinary fool that has no more brain than a stone … '

'Oh, you are sick of self-love, Malvolio,' Olivia interrupted him, laughing at him now. 'You taste with a sick appetite … '

She paused: the sound of raised voices had reached them, above all the boisterous tones of Sir Toby Belch.

Maria hurried in. There was, it seemed, a young gentleman at the gate determined to speak to Olivia.

Olivia sighed. Most probably another messenger from Orsino. She despatched Maria to rescue the messenger from Sir Toby's hospitality, for she could be fairly certain her uncle would be spouting drunken idiocies, and sent Malvolio to turn the

messenger away. Any excuse would do, she was ill
or not at home, anything, to rid her of this
unwelcome intrusion.

It seemed, however, that not even Malvolio's
disdainful nose could block the persistent young
man. He was, it seemed, fortified against any denial.

Curious despite herself, Olivia enquired, 'What
kind of man is he?'

'Why, of mankind,' Malvolio assured her pompously.

Olivia tried again. 'What does he look like? How
old is he?'

Malvolio considered this question with some care,
pursing his lips and flaring his nostrils with the effort
of estimating the possible worth of such a person in
Malvolio's ranks of men …

'Not yet old enough for a man, nor young enough
for a boy,' he announced. 'As an unripe peapod
before it is a … peapod,' he continued, 'or an unripe
apple when it is almost an apple. It is, with him, like
at the turn of the tide, between boy and man … '

Malvolio had quite lost himself in the intricacies of
these poetic images … Olivia gave up. And then,

more from boredom than anything else, she succumbed to an unexpected curiosity. She would let this messenger in, just to have a look at him.

'Give me my veil,' she told Maria. 'Throw it over my face.'

Unaware of the stir he had created in this household so firmly barred against all visitors, the stranger marched in with a stride a little too consciously masterful and a voice a little too determinedly low; for the 'he' was not a he at all; it was a she … It was Viola, disguised as Cesario, the love-sick duke's new page.

Faced suddenly with two unknown young women, Viola paused and stared from one to the other.

'The honourable lady of the house, which is she?' she asked.

'Speak to me; I shall answer for her,' Olivia murmured from behind the veil. But though her tone suggested she was but slightly interested, a peep behind that lacy mask would have revealed another tale. Lady Olivia, mourning or otherwise, was not immune to the charms of so handsome a young man as this 'gentleman' who stood before her now.

Viola drew a deep breath and unfolded the paper on which she had written her speech. She was determined to discharge her task for her beloved duke as faithfully as she was able.

'Most radiant, exquisite and unmatchable beauty,' she began in ringing tones, but hearing a smothered titter from Maria, she halted. She looked from Maria to the veiled lady reclining gracefully on a chair.

'I pray you, tell me if this be the lady of the house, for I never saw her,' she said to Maria. 'I would be loath to cast away my speech, for besides being excellently written, I have taken great pains to learn it.'

'Where do you come from, sir?' enquired Olivia haughtily, intrigued against her better judgement by this earnest, though somewhat cheeky, persistence.

'I can say little more than I have studied,' protested Viola. She was frustrated by her inability to get on with the task in hand and return as fast as possible to Duke Orsino's side. 'Are you the lady of the house?'

And to be truthful, she was feeling rather angry.
Here was this beautiful woman supposedly in
mourning, yet behaving with an unseemly coquettish
tilt to her graceful head, and apparently playing
games with her, while Duke Orsino languished in
misery for want of love.

'Speak,' sighed Olivia, seeing now that this young
man could not be turned from his declared purpose.

Viola took a deep breath and launched, 'Most
sweet lady … '

But two more interruptions from Olivia, and Viola
saw that no suit from Duke Orsino would ever
penetrate this woman's heart. She stared at her in
miserable disbelief. Here was a woman who had the
hand and heart of Duke Orsino for the asking, yet
she spurned it. What was she like, this lady made
of stone?

'Good madam,' she said suddenly, growing bold,
'let me see your face.'

'Have you a mission from your lord to negotiate
with my face?' Olivia enquired softly. But the request
had pleased her, for this youth (or so she thought he

was) absorbed her more and more with every passing minute that he stood there earnest, honest, protesting for his lord.

'But we will draw the curtain and show you the picture,' she said. Slowly, she lifted the veil and showed her exquisite face. 'Is it not well done?' she enquired, with a gleam of mockery in her dark eyes.

'Excellently done … if God did all,' murmured Viola, at the same time admiring the flawless beauty displayed before her, and with a woman's discerning (and perhaps a little jealous) eye, searching for the touches of artistry that might give a bloom to cheeks and lips …

'It will endure wind and weather,' Olivia assured her, aware only that her face had made some impression on this handsome youth, and interpreting it as the palpitations of a beating heart much like that thundering in her own breast now.

'It is true beauty,' murmured Viola, searching the face Orsino loved so passionately. She saw the arch looks and the saucy smiles being thrown towards her; her sorrow for the scorned duke and for herself, prevented by her disguise from ever seeking Orsino's love, sent a hot flush of anger to her cheeks.

'If I did love you with my master's flame, with such a suffering, such a deadly life, I would find no sense in your denial; I would not understand it,' she pleaded.

'What would you do?' Olivia whispered, her eyes fixed on the youth's face. It seemed to have grown more handsome than ever before as he spoke again of his master's love.

'I would make me a willow cabin at your gate, and call upon my soul within the house; write songs of love and sing them even in the dead of night; cry out your name to the echoing hills and make the whispers of the air murmur "Olivia"! Oh, you should not rest between the elements of air and earth, but you should pity me!'

For a long moment, Olivia sat looking at Viola's passionate face. It was as though her eyes were fastened by some magic to this youth and would never leave again.

Then she realized the look of fascination that must

be showing on her face, and she dropped her eyes hurriedly, her cheeks colouring with sudden shame.

'You might do much,' she said, slowly, but she was talking to herself; for while the past half hour had started as a game, in boredom, and had continued as a tantalizing teasing of this youth, it had become now something else. Olivia was listening to echoes within her heart that she had never heard before, echoes that she had vowed she would never hear till seven long years of mourning had gone by, echoes that she had believed she could not hear, for misery at her beloved brother's death.

This youth, entering her life merely as another's messenger, seemed to carry messages of another sort which tapped these slumbering echoes …

She tried to gather her composure. 'Get you to your lord,' she murmured, quietly now. 'I cannot love him; let him send no more … '

And then a sudden flare of daring took her again, and almost before she had realized what she said, she added hastily, 'Unless, perhaps, you come to me again … to tell me how he takes it. Fare you well.'

Behind the departing Viola's back, Olivia sat for a moment without moving. She could hear nothing but her thundering heart, feel nothing but the hot flush flooding her cheeks, see nothing but the vision of that handsome face ingrained for ever on her memory.

Almost before she knew what she was doing, she called Malvolio to her, pulling her ring off her finger, and holding it out to him.

'Run after that same peevish messenger, the duke's man,' she said, with a feigned air of carelessness. 'He left this ring behind.' She almost blushed at the lie, but Malvolio's nose had risen so high in the air at the sight of the disdained ring, that he was unaware of any tell-tale colours on his mistress's cheek.

'Tell him I'll have none of it,' ended Olivia hastily. 'Tell him not to flatter his lord, nor hold him up with hopes of my love; I am not for him; and,' she turned away, lest even Malvolio should see the flush rising across her face, 'if that youth will come this way tomorrow, I'll give him reasons for it.'

Nursing the ring gingerly as though it reeked of

the scorned suitor, Malvolio marched out to do his
mistress's will ...

Two men were striding along a footpath
that crossed a rocky head-land. One, the
elder, was speaking warmly, urgently, to
the younger man who seemed to shake his head and
plead a little with his companion ...

To the observer who had just seen Viola dressed as
Cesario march angrily from Olivia's house, the sight
of what appeared to be Cesario here, high on a rocky
headland on the other side of Illyria, would have
caused more than a little confusion.

At closer glance, the observer might have noticed
that Cesario had changed his clothes and was not
wearing the finery of a duke's page, that his face was
somewhat squarer, giving the appearance of being
larger, and from time to time he wore a cap. (No one
had ever yet seen Cesario without his cap, for the
simple reason that without his cap, Cesario would
have betrayed the rich tresses of a girl's fair hair.)

This Cesario had short-cropped hair, and was altogether broader, his frame much squarer …

And this was hardly surprising, for this was not Cesario, Viola disguised as Orsino's page. This was her brother, her twin, Sebastian, whom she believed was dead. A youth so like his sister that they were almost two peas in the same pod that had so preoccupied Malvolio …

Shortly after his sister had safely reached the shore, Sebastian had been pulled from the waves by Antonio, the man who walked beside him now, protesting.

Their argument was simple: Antonio had grown to love this youth whose life he'd saved. He wanted Sebastian to stay.

Sebastian, on the other hand, was all for moving on. He was filled with gratitude and affection for Antonio's kindness, but he was also too well aware of how his sorrows for his sister (for he believed that she was dead) would make him always a burden to this kind man. His intention was to travel on, as fancy took him. If he stayed, tears and misery would constantly overwhelm him and he did not wish to impose his unhappiness on Antonio.

He had decided he would visit Duke Orsino's court, to see what time and fate might offer …

Antonio was a sea-faring man and had, in past sea-battles with Orsino's fleet, made enemies at Orsino's court: going there would be unsafe for him. Yet watching Sebastian stride away, his love for the impetuous youth was stronger than any fears for his own safety … He threw all care to the winds and set off to keep Sebastian company, wherever his adventures might take him.

Viola knew nothing of her brother's miraculous presence in this land. She knew only that misery seemed to grow around her by the minute. Not only was she mourning a brother's death, but she was compelled to love a man who neither loved her, nor even knew she was a woman! She was compelled to carry messages of *his* love to another woman! And this woman was as hard-hearted as she was beautiful.

Now, to crown the sorry tale, here was that same Olivia's steward pursuing her from the house, his thumb and forefinger pinched together, disdainfully holding out a ring as if it were tainted with some unmentionable disease. And now he informed her that Olivia 'returned' the ring!

'If it be worth stooping for, there it lies … if not, let it be his that finds it,' intoned Malvolio, opening his fingers and letting the offending jewel drop to the ground. It rolled in a circle and stopped at Viola's feet. Malvolio swung on his heel and swept away.

Viola stared at the ring. 'I left no ring with her: what does this lady mean?'

But even as Malvolio disappeared from sight an awful thought entered Viola's mind. She bent down and picked up Olivia's ring. She held it cautiously in the palm of her hand. Could this be intended as a love token? Could her appearance, her *disguised* appearance, have charmed the lady into loving her, believing her to be a man?

The appalling thought was more awful than her wildest nightmares: 'My master loves her dearly; and I love him as much; and she, mistaken, seems to dote on me!' She pondered this circle of misery with dismay. 'What will become of this?' As long as she pretended to be a man, she would remain desperate for her master's love; yet as she was truly a woman, how many purposeless sighs would poor Olivia have to breathe for love of that non-existent youth, Cesario!

'Oh, time,' sighed Viola despairingly, 'you must untangle this, not I. It is too hard a knot for me to untie.'

Sir Toby Belch was in fine form. It was long past midnight: quantities of wine and most delicious food had been consumed, and still more was to be had; and he began to thump a rhythm with his boot and tankard, while Sir Andrew Aguecheek trilled merrily after him, and Feste the jester's considerably more musical tones rounded the whole thing off into the most jovial of uproars.

The rest of the household, sensibly fast asleep, could not remain so for long. Maria was the first to appear, hastily pulling on her dressing-gown.

'What a caterwauling do you keep here!' she cried. 'If my lady has not called up her steward Malvolio and bid him turn you out of doors, never trust me!'

For answer, Sir Toby seized the irate maid by the waist and waltzed her to and fro.

'O, the twelfth day of December … ' he carolled.

'For the love of God, peace!' pleaded Maria, half-laughing now. And then she stopped.

An apparition was at the door. A long white nightgown, crowned by a long white nightcap which in turn framed a long white face crumpled with such disdain, disgust and horror that it must surely cripple any man for life to be so burdened with it.

It was Malvolio. He halted. He surveyed the assembled company. He allowed his eyes to come to rest finally, reluctantly, on Sir Toby Belch.

'My masters, are you mad or what are you?' he

34

enquired in a voice shrill with affronted anger. 'Have you no wit, manners, nor honesty, but to gabble like tinkers at this time of night? Is there no respect of place, persons, nor time in you?'

'We did keep time, sir, in our songs,' retorted Sir Toby, and he thumped his knee in pleasure at this last fine gem of wit.

'Sir Toby,' shrieked Malvolio in rage. 'My lady bid me tell you that, though she harbours you as her kinsman, she's not attached to your misbehaviour. If you can separate yourself and your behaviour, you are welcome to the house; if not, she is willing to bid you farewell.'

For answer Sir Toby burst forth into song, and was joined by Feste the jester, who paid no respects to any man, least of all to disgruntled household stewards who disapproved …

'Do you think,' Sir Toby thrust his face so close to the offended steward that Malvolio was forced to step hastily back for fear of being stifled by the fumes of ale. 'Do you think that because *you* are virtuous, there shall be no more cakes and ale?'

Malvolio had no answer. With a look of pure hatred that engulfed them all, the steward strode out, his nose higher than ever, his night cap swinging like the bell of doom, and his voice muttering darkly that Lady Olivia would hear of this …

Had not Maria held Sir Toby back, the infuriated man might well have rolled after Malvolio and boxed his ears into oblivion, for in all the rumpus Sir Toby had heard nothing of Olivia's pleas for good behaviour in her house; he heard only the insolent, offensive, always disapproving tones of Malvolio, whose gloomy face and appalling vanity seemed to bring the only cloud on to Sir Toby's jovial horizon, but a cloud that was always there.

'Sweet Sir Toby, be patient for tonight,' urged Maria. She had come herself in irritation at the noise made by Sir Toby and his fellow revellers; but in an instant this had been transformed by Malvolio's sour face into a burning desire to teach the acid-tongued steward a lesson, to find some sweet revenge …

'Since the youth of the duke was with my lady, she is much disturbed,' she warned Sir Toby Belch. 'As for Monsieur Malvolio, leave him to me … '

Sir Toby saw that some plan was taking shape in her sharp brain. In gleeful anticipation, he wrapped his arms about her robust waist, and planted an exuberant kiss on both her cheeks.

With a laughing tap on his nose, Maria swung herself free, and clapped her hands for their attention. The plan was in her mind, perfect … 'I will drop in his way some obscure letters of love,' she told her attentive audience, 'where, by the colour of his beard, the shape of his leg, the manner of his walk, the expression of his eyes, forehead and complexion, he shall find himself most accurately described. I can write very like my lady, your niece … '

'Excellent! I smell a trick!' Sir Toby slapped his knee in pure delight.

'I have it in my nose too!' chortled Sir Andrew Aguecheek …

'And he shall think,' Toby's brain was far from slow, and in that instant he had seen Maria's brilliant device, 'he shall think, by the letters you will drop, that they come from my niece and that she's in love with him!' He bellowed in ecstasy at the thought of any temptation to Malvolio's disgusting vanity.

'I will hide you two where he shall find the letter,' Maria assured them. 'Observe what he makes of it!' She wagged her finger at the drunken pair. 'For this night, to bed, and dream on the event!'

'Come, come, I'll go drink some sherry; it is too late to go to bed now,' declared Sir Toby. He wrapped his arm around the swaying Sir Andrew's shoulders. 'Come, knight! Come, knight!'

Duke Orsino was talking of love. 'If ever you love, in the sweet pangs of it, remember me,' he told 'Cesario', whose attentive ear provided him with greater comfort than he had ever had. Once more he had been rejected by Olivia. Once more he languished in the misery of unrequited love.

Orsino looked searchingly at Viola, though he saw no more than the figure of his faithful page Cesario and not the face of a woman who adored him more with every minute that she spent by his side. 'Young though you are, your eye has strayed upon some person that it loves, has it not, boy?' he enquired, gently and with a fatherly expression in his eyes.

'A little,' admitted Viola.

'What kind of woman is it?' the duke enquired.

'Of your complexion,' Viola replied, with beating heart.

'She is not worth you, then,' the duke dismissed this. 'And how old?'

'About your age, my lord,' Viola whispered, and looked with scarcely disguised longing into his face …

Orsino, of course, did not see that tell-tale lustre in her eyes. His thoughts had moved again to Olivia, and poor Viola was once more to be no more than his messenger to that lady, carrying further words of Orsino's undying love.

'But if she cannot love you, sir,' Viola protested, frustrated with this thankless task and distressed that she would be again the bearer of such hurtful news to this man that she adored.

'I cannot accept that answer,' Orsino pushed the thought away.

'But you must!' persisted Viola. 'Say that some lady, as perhaps there is,' she wondered if the flush colouring her cheeks could be seen by Duke Orsino, 'say that some lady has for your love as great a pang of heart as you have for Olivia: you cannot love her; you tell her so; must she not then be answered?'

'There is no woman's heart can hold the beating of so strong a passion as love gives to my heart,' cried the heart-sick duke. 'Make no comparison between the love a woman can bear me and that I owe Olivia!'

'Aye, but I know … ' Viola burst out, in misery.

'What do you know?' enquired the duke.

Viola was so close to spilling out her love for him, that in a moment she would have plunged across the precipice. 'Too well what love women may bear for men,' she cried. 'My father had a daughter loved a man, as might be … perhaps, … were I a woman … I should love your lordship … '

The duke looked at his earnest page with some

amusement. He put an arm about the young lad's shoulders, 'And what's her history?'

Viola lowered her eyes, afraid that he would see the light of love in them. 'A blank, my lord,' she murmured. 'She never told her love, but let concealment, like a worm in the bud, feed on her damask cheek: she pined in thought, and with a green and yellow melancholy she sat like patience on a monument, smiling at grief … '

And she smiled up at him, mistress of her unruly emotions once again. 'Was this not love indeed?'

'But did your sister die of her love, my boy?' the duke persisted, intrigued by this melancholy tale.

'I am all the daughters of my father's house … ' whispered Viola almost lost again, and teetering on the brink of telling all … 'and all the brothers too … ' she ended hastily. She turned from him, quickly composing her face as was more fitting for the servant of a noble duke. 'Sir, shall I to this lady?'

'Aye, that's the theme. To her in haste,' Orsino urged. 'Give her this jewel, say my love can give no place, waits no denial … '

The letter glinted, tantalizing in the morning sun. Behind the exuberant blooms of a large flowering bush, three figures crouched, though there could be nothing secret about their presence there. Sir Toby chortled, Sir Andrew cackled, and Fabian, another of Olivia's servants, hissed and hushed at them both. To any other person walking in that sunlit garden, the dishevelled, boisterous trio would have been instantly visible.

But not to Malvolio. Malvolio was busy. Malvolio was deep in a most exquisite fantasy. Malvolio was not Malvolio, Olivia's servant, but Malvolio, a great and powerful nobleman ... and Malvolio had been practising a nobleman's behaviour to his own shadow for the past half hour. Indeed Malvolio was quite lost in this inspiring vision of himself. He addressed the trees, the sky, the sun, and all were courtiers to him ...

'To be Count Malvolio,' he said, rolling the words around his tongue, 'having been three months married to Olivia ... calling my

43

officers about me,' he waved a peremptory hand towards the trees, 'in my branched velvet gown, having come from a day-bed where I have left Olivia sleeping … '

'Fire and brimstone!' spluttered Sir Toby Belch, and nearly fell out of the bush. He was yanked back out of sight by Fabian.

'Telling them … ' Malvolio smirked at the thought of this next vision, 'telling them, I know my place as I wish them to know theirs … to ask for my kinsman, Toby … '

'Belts and shackles!' this time Sir Toby exploded from the bush, and had to be hauled back by the combined strengths of Fabian and Sir Andrew …

Malvolio's fantasy continued. 'I frown the while,' the sky was withered by his frown, 'perchance wind up my watch or play with … some rich jewel; Toby approaches; curtsies there to me … ' Malvolio's face took on an air of pained dignity. He held a hand out to the imaginary Toby. 'I extend my hand to him thus, quenching my familiar smile with an austere regard of control … '

44

'And does not Toby give you a blow on the lips then?' shrieked Toby, muzzled instantly by Fabian, who was determined to see out this escapade, for he too had fallen foul of Malvolio's pinch-faced disapproval and felt that a ripe punishment for such a man would be a good day's work.

But now Malvolio's prancing feet had neared the letter that lay in wait for him. It was Maria's letter, faking the handwriting of Olivia, and laid carefully on the path for him to find …

'By my life, this is my lady's writing!' exclaimed Malvolio on cue. He unfolded the paper, carefully, and paying little attention to the possibility that such a letter might be private to her ladyship, began to read. 'Jove knows I love: but who? Lips do not move; no man must know,' he read the tantalizing words aloud. And then a thought struck him. Transfixed, he stood there, clasping the letter to his chest, his face suddenly aflame with knowledge. If these words should be for him!

The watchers tittered. Could the man truly be so

easily caught? A riddle, a few clues (some of the letters of Malvolio's name, which his brain deciphered slowly), and Maria's trap was set: Malvolio was utterly convinced the letter was from Olivia, writing in secret, to him.

He read on. 'If this fall into your hands, revolve.' Malvolio spun on his heels. 'In my stars I am above you.' He looked up. And then he understood the clue and drew a deep breath of pure, glorious satisfaction. Of course! *Lady* Olivia was of noble birth, and so above him. He returned with rapt attention to the letter: 'but be not afraid of greatness,' it went on. 'Some are born great, some achieve greatness, and some have greatness thrust upon them … Remember who commended your yellow stockings, and wished to see you always cross-gartered … If you return my love, let it appear in your smiling; your smiles become you well; therefore in my presence smile, dear my sweet, I beg you … '

Malvolio stood in silence, gazing at the glorious letter. Then he clasped it to his bosom. He raised his eyes to heaven. 'I will smile!' he cried, 'I will do everything that you wish!' and in a paroxysm of delight he rushed away, to clad himself in the yellow stockings and cross-garters, and to prepare the smile that would eclipse all smiles, for Olivia …

Unable to control their mirth any longer, Sir Toby, Fabian and Sir Andrew fell out of the bush, and rolled across the path, stopping only when Maria appeared, eager to know if her letter had achieved the desired effect.

'Why, you have put him in such a dream,' gasped Sir Toby Belch, 'that when the image of it leaves him he must run mad!'

'If you will then see the fruits of this sport,' Maria interrupted her fellow plotters' raucous laughter, 'mark his first approach before my lady: he will come to her in yellow stockings, and … ' she snorted with laughter, 'it is a colour she loathes; and cross-gartered, a fashion she detests; and he will smile upon her, which will now be so unsuitable to her mood … !'

Viola's discomfort was growing by the minute. Once more forced to visit Olivia on behalf of Duke Orsino, she must endure not merely her master's rejection, but now an open wooing of herself! Olivia, by turns made shy or bold as the throbs of love filled her with courage or plunged her into abject shame, now declared her love for Orsino's page!

'Cesario, by the roses of the spring, by maidhood, honour, truth and everything, I love you so!' she cried. 'In spite of all your pride, neither wit nor reason can hide my passion.'

'By innocence I swear, and by my youth, I have one heart, one bosom and one truth, and that no woman has,' Viola cried. What was she to do in this extraordinary predicament? Such ardent sighs from Lady Olivia! Such gleaming eyes! Such longing hand-clasps, from which Viola escaped only with difficulty. 'Nor shall anyone be mistress of my heart except I alone,' she protested frantically. 'And so, farewell, good madam!'

This must, she promised herself, be absolutely

the last visit to the countess for her master. She could endure this miserable confusion for not a minute more!

Sir Andrew Aguecheek was most unhappy. He had seen the countess pay more attention in a few moments to the duke's new page than she had paid in *weeks* to hopeful Andrew Aguecheek.

And with this he had finally seen enough. He would not stay a moment longer!

Sir Toby was made suddenly aware that the fat purse that lined their days with comforts was about to be whisked beyond his reach. Instantly, Sir Toby and Fabian were awash with words of hearty encouragement: the problem (as they put it to the disappointed knight) was that Olivia was watching to see how Sir Andrew would perform against this upstart page. The answer to the problem lay simply in challenging Cesario to a duel. Would not such a duel be closely watched by Lady Olivia? Was she not plainly eager to know how her favoured suitor, good Sir Andrew, would fare!

So was the pouting Sir Andrew transformed again. He set off, much cheered, to write his challenge to the page who dared to try to claim Olivia's heart from him!

Sebastian and Antonio had at last arrived in town. Antonio, concerned not to be seen by any who would recognize him, had gone straight to find them lodgings in the suburbs and arranged to meet Sebastian there later. Sebastian set off to wander curiously around the town, to look at the sights for which the place was famed, and do a little shopping with the money which good Antonio had left him for his use, stowed safely in Antonio's own purse.

Meanwhile Olivia had sent for Cesario again. She waited nervously for the arrival of this youth, for she was by now so deeply in love with him that her whole existence seemed to hang on her adoration of him. She had forgotten what it was once like not to know him or to love him.

She waited, pacing before the door, wringing her hands, straightening her hair, her skirt ... how exactly should she behave towards Cesario? What could she do to win his love?

For her pains, she got not Cesario, but Malvolio. And what a Malvolio! Brilliant in sunshine-yellow stockings, like some gigantic stalking bird, his legs laced most exotically with intricate cross-gartering, a smile from ear to ear like an enormous wound from which his teeth loomed, glistening ... and such a wealth of knowing nods and winks, and kissing hands towards Olivia ...

Olivia drew back in horror, quite unprepared for this transformation of her sober steward. Was this the man she relied on utterly to maintain the calm and smooth-running of a sombre house of mourning? The poor man must be dreadfully ill!

And there he was, leering and winking again, while all the while the strangest of words dropped

from his ever-smiling mouth ...

'Be not afraid of greatness!' he grinned grotesquely at Olivia and twirled a shapely yellow-gartered leg; 'it was well written,' he assured her. 'Some are born great, some achieve greatness ... ' he pranced before her, his smile stretching till it seemed to split his face in two. Then, with a string of wild flourishes with one flapping hand, he bent low before Olivia, to grimace ludicrously into her startled face, 'and some have greatness thrust upon them!' he finished, with a knowing wink.

Olivia, of course, knew nothing of the fake letter which had provided Malvolio's guide for this inspired performance. These antics from her usually impeccable steward were beyond her comprehension. There was no explanation for it but that the poor, blighted man had gone quite mad. With news of Cesario's arrival distracting her, she hastily gave orders that Malvolio should be taken care of, for she would not have harm come to him for all the world ...

So it was that Sir Toby came to be entrusted with

the care of 'mad' Malvolio! What a perfect place from which to exact revenge ... and what a revenge it proved to be!

If Malvolio was behaving in a fashion for which the only explanation was his madness, why then mad he would be called, and with what gusto did Sir Toby, Sir Andrew, Fabian and Feste enter into this scheme of Malvolio's madness. Malvolio could not open his mouth, but that his audience squealed at the poor man's confusion of wit, he could not utter a single sound, but that they berated the 'foul fiends and devils' which had taken possession of his soul ... And the more they baited Malvolio, the angrier, ruder, and more arrogant the man became, for had not the letter also said he should deal roughly with servants, rudely with kinsman ...?

It all fitted so perfectly with Malvolio's expectations, and the letter had stroked his vanity with such audacity, that he followed, nose up in the air, right into the trap without a suspicion in the world that this was anything other than the device by which his mistress wished to show her secret love for him and urge him to show his love for her!

Sir Toby in revenge was ruthless. In a trice he had confined his victim in a pitch-dark room, bound hand and foot for being a madman, there to endure his plight until such time as Toby might feel pity for the man …

Meanwhile Sir Toby's main concern was to keep Sir Andrew and his purse firmly in Olivia's house.

That hopeful knight had valiantly struggled off to write a challenge to 'Cesario'. He returned with some writing which was as addled as his meagre brain. This prize he entrusted proudly to Sir Toby, to be conveyed with all due ceremony to Cesario.

Behind his back, Sir Toby and Fabian were quick to hide what Sir Andrew had written. If Cesario should read this missive from the 'challenger', he could not help but see the towering heights of idiocy, not bravery, that spurred on the aged knight who dared him to a duel.

Instead, Sir Toby waylaid Cesario and most eloquently conveyed Sir Andrew's challenge by word of mouth. So vivid was the report of Sir Andrew Aguecheek's bravery and skill, his fury, deadly speed and daring, that it would have sent any youth into a state of nervousness over the safety of his life. It sent Cesario into a state of abject terror, for Viola had never even held a weapon in her hand and possessed neither the slightest skill, nor any will to fight. The prospect of duels, blood and death merely curdled her brain, transformed her strong straight legs into trembling pins that buckled at the knees, her arms into quivering rubber that had no strength even to hold the offending sword, and her voice, which she normally succeeded in pitching low enough to have some semblance of a young man's tones, to a pitiful squeak … the more so because the poor girl did not have the faintest idea what should have caused such anger against her.

All her efforts to escape the duel only caught her faster in the trap: according to Sir Toby

Belch, a knight like fierce Sir Andrew Aguecheek
would let no one rest until his challenge had
been answered ...

Returning as swiftly as his bloated bulk allowed, Sir
Toby filled Sir Andrew's reeling head with terrors of
a similar sort. This page of Duke Orsino's was a very
devil! Such a skill with swords! There was no peace to
be made with such a man: nothing but a duel to the
death would satisfy him!

Sir Andrew swayed and would have fainted,
but Sir Toby marched the wilting knight towards
his doom ...

His doom, in the shape of Viola praying that the
ground would open up and swallow her, grew deathly
pale. She beheld this bringer of destruction march
towards her, and saw he was held back from his thirst
for blood only by the sheer strength of his two
companions! She trembled, and clutched at the
sword Toby had thrust into her hands ...

'Put up your sword!' the fierce cry seemed to come
from nowhere, and like a thunderbolt from heaven,
a man leapt out in front of her, his broad shape

blocking off the waving sword of Andrew Aguecheek. 'If this young gentleman has done offence, I take the fault on me,' he shouted at the knight. 'If you offend *him*, I defy you for him!' and standing belligerently before Viola, the stranger held his own weapon menacingly, daring anyone to move towards her …

The speed with which her fate had been transformed from certain death to daring rescue by a total stranger was too much for Viola. Relief and shock flooded over her and turned her legs to water …

Who was this man? She had never seen him before, nor the soldiers who burst in and set upon her saviour, and had him bound between two stout guards before she had even recovered from the last shock. Arrested! By Duke Orsino's men!

And there was more. Now this stranger turned a look of love on her, and in a gruff, gentle voice, spoke as though he knew her!

'This comes with seeking you,' Antonio said, for Viola's rescuer was none other than this loyal friend of her own brother, Sebastian. And Antonio looked

with sorrow on the youth that he had just rescued, whom he believed was Sebastian. 'But my necessity makes me ask you for my purse … '

Purse? She had no purse of his! Viola began to wonder now if she was going mad.

Antonio halted, having seen her look of blank denial. He searched her face. A look of disbelieving horror crept across it. Denied! Thrown off when most he needed help! He tried again. 'I must ask you for some of that money.'

'What money, sir?' Viola asked in all innocence. 'For the fair kindness you have showed me here, I'll lend you something!'

He appealed in desperation to the soldiers who still held him fast. 'This youth that you see here I snatched one half out of the jaws of death … But oh how vile an idol is this god! Sebastian …!'

Sebastian! Viola's mind could barely hold the word. This man mistook her for another called Sebastian! A surge of thoughts rushed through her head: her own brother Sebastian looked very much like she did … even his clothes would be a little like the ones she wore, for it was Sebastian's style that she had followed in making up her page's clothes ...

Could this stranger's Sebastian be her own brother? Could brother Sebastian be, after all these months, alive?

Sebastian, ignorant of the grim fate that had befallen his good friend Antonio, and still wandering idly about the town, filled up his time with small activities to erase the misery that filled his heart at memories of his sister's death.

Imagine then his irritation when he was accosted by a cheeky jester who claimed to know him well, and claimed he had been sent to find him by his mistress!

'Go to, you are a foolish fellow,' Sebastian retorted. 'Let me be rid of you.'

'No, I do not know you,' Feste mocked, for it was he. 'Nor am I sent to you by my lady to bid you come and speak with her; nor your name is not Master

Cesario; nor this is not my nose, neither. Nothing that is so is so!'

'I beg you, vent your folly somewhere else. You do not know me,' Sebastian dismissed him.

But hardly had he turned from this than he was set upon by a great beanpole of a gentleman who waved a sword as though it were a wand and stabbed the air with it, egged on by a monstrous, bloated wine-barrel of a man …

'Are all the people mad?' Sebastian yelled, drawing his sword to defend himself, and dealing the prancing knight a solid, no-nonsense blow.

Sir Andrew, who had been hit in the arm, and Sir Toby who had been hit nowhere but in his expectations that they were going to thrash their victim soundly, … stared in some confusion at the youth they thought was young Cesario. What, quaking at the knees a moment ago when the soldiers came, and now no less than a raging tiger of a man! Incensed, Sir Toby grabbed Sir Andrew's sword …

'Hold, Toby; on your life, I charge you, hold!'

Olivia's furious voice rang out and stopped even Sir Toby in his bull-like rush towards his quarry.

'Ungracious wretch,' she hurled at him. 'Out of my sight!' Then she turned with such a glow of love towards Sebastian. 'Be not offended, dear Cesario,' she calmed him, and her tones were golden honey with the warmth of adoration in them.

Sebastian stood rooted to the ground in wonderment, disbelief and awe (tinged with an adventurer's lightning flash of insight at his miraculous good fortune). Apparently there was one Cesario much sought after in these parts, and much beloved by this jewel of a lady! Apparently he, Sebastian, was being mistaken for this Cesario. So either *they* were mad, or *he* was mad, or else this was a dream; and if it was a dream, why then, let him sleep on ...

While all the world ran circles round Sebastian, believing him to be Cesario, and Antonio was arrested defending

Cesario, believing him to be Sebastian, Malvolio was still shut away and treated as a madman by Sir Toby and his accomplices.

Now they persuaded Feste to dress up in a gown and beard and go to him: adopting a priest's solemn, sing-song tones, Feste duly hailed Malvolio through the tiny window of his dismal prison.

From inside there came the startled cry 'Who calls there?'

'Sir Topas the priest, who comes to visit Malvolio the lunatic,' intoned Feste the jester.

'Sir Topas, Sir Topas, good Sir Topas, go to my lady,' pleaded Malvolio, the hood-winked steward. 'Never was a man thus wronged: good Sir Topas do not think me mad: they have laid me here in hideous darkness!' and at this last the poor man's voice quite broke with the horror and the terror of his plight.

Listening, even Sir Toby felt a twinge of some regret, though it was less for Malvolio's plight than for his own.

'Go to him in your own voice,' he urged Feste,

'bring me word how you find him. I wish we were well rid of this joke. If he could be conveniently released, I wish he were, for I am now so far out of favour with my niece that I cannot go any further with this sport … '

The familiar tones of Feste the jester reached Malvolio in his darkened cell and new hope surged through his black despair.

'Good fool,' he begged the jester with a respect he had never used before to him, 'Good fool, help me to a candle, pen, ink and paper: as I am a gentleman, I will live to be thankful to you for it.'

'Master Malvolio?' Feste enquired, with mock surprise.

'They keep me in darkness and do all they can to keep me out of my wits,' Malvolio cried. 'Good fool, help me to some light and some paper,' he repeated his pitiful refrain. 'I tell you, I am as well in my wits as any man in Illyria … '

On the question of how mad or sane were the people of Illyria, Sebastian at least would have been hard put to give a clear reply. Here was he, snatched from the jaws of death, plunged deep in sorrow for his sister's death, transported suddenly into a world of glory where the most exquisite lady (a countess, no less, and wealthy, too) adored him …

'This is the air; that is the glorious sun,' he told himself. 'This pearl she gave me, I do feel it and see it; and though it is wonder that surrounds me, yet it is not madness.' But then again, could he be certain of that?

And where was Antonio? His disappearance was bewildering. Sebastian had looked in vain for him at their arranged meeting place. Antonio had indeed been there, and had after scoured the town searching for Sebastian. But since, the man had disappeared!

And even as he pondered this strangest of strange accidents which brought him into the arms of this exquisite lady, Olivia herself appeared. She brought a priest with her, and now she begged Cesario (for so she believed Sebastian to be), to vow before the priest that he would marry her!

She stared breathlessly at Sebastian, in that instant suddenly appalled at her own audacity …

'What do you say?' she whispered, hardly daring to hear Cesario's answer. How little time had passed since she pursued Cesario with little encouragement to love, and yet how swiftly his cool rejection had become an ardent passion …

Now, waiting nervously for his reply, her fears were swiftly put to rest. 'Cesario' clasped her to his heart, and answered, 'I'll go with you; and having sworn truth, ever will be true.'

The Duke Orsino could stand no more rejection from Olivia. For months he had sung of his love by letter, messenger, gifts, poems, and nothing had won her heart. Now he came himself.

And Viola came too, nervous for her lord and for herself … she dared not think what might happen next!

What was to become of this appalling tangle of events? Orsino loved a woman, who loved Orsino's page, who was a woman hiding as a man, who loved Orsino …

They got no further than Olivia's garden.

'Here comes the man, sir, that rescued me!' Viola cried, relieved that she could show her saviour to the duke, for he alone could release Antonio from his guards.

The duke eyed the man slowly. 'That face I do remember well, yet when I saw it last, it was besmeared in the smoke of war … ' he told Viola. 'He was the captain of a vessel that grappled with the most noble ship of our fleet … '

'He did me kindness, sir, drew his weapon in my defence, though in doing so he spoke so strangely … '

Antonio had been standing there, his dark eyes fixed in smouldering defiance on Viola. This final

betrayal was too much for him. 'Orsino, noble sir,'
he burst out, 'that most ungrateful boy there by your
side … ' in a fury of hurt he poured out his tale: how
he had snatched the youth from raging seas, had
brought him back to life and grown to love him …
how he had thrown all care to the winds to follow
him, protect him, care for him … for which he had
received only betrayal, denial, and the crowning
insult … 'he even denied me my own purse which I
gave him for his use not half an hour before!'

'When did he come to this town?' Orsino asked,
intrigued, for clearly the man spoke with an honest
belief in the truth of his own tale.

'Today, my lord,' Antonio replied, 'and for three
months before, both day and night, we did keep
company.'

'Fellow, your words are madness,' the duke assured
him, 'for three months this youth has waited upon
me … ' but even this engaging mystery was put to
sudden flight from Orsino's mind, for Olivia had
entered the room, and Orsino had no eyes for
anyone else.

Olivia, however, had no eyes for any but Cesario. Though she was courteous enough in greeting to the duke, her gaze was fastened only on his page.

'Cesario, you do not keep promise with me,' she challenged, with a look of hurt.

The duke heard this at first with incomprehension. But having once again tried to gain Olivia's attention and found it was locked fast on young Cesario, a new thought entered the rejected lover's brain. It was Cesario the lady loved! This final rejection was more than he could stand; he could be as cruel as she! He would take away this youth that she adored, to spite her love …

Now Olivia saw her passionate lover of a few hours ago, willingly prepared to go off with the duke!

'Where does Cesario go?' she cried.

'After him I love more than I love these eyes, more than my life, more than ever I shall love a wife,' Viola declared, throwing all caution off, and turning ardently towards her lord.

Orsino looked at her in some surprise. This passion, though he knew the youth was fond of him, was not expected. Viola, feeling her loved one's searching eyes on her, raised hers and met his gaze, then in confusion flushed deep red …

'Cesario, husband, stay,' shrieked Olivia.

'Husband!' yelled the duke. Betrayed by his page!

This appalling truth was instantly confirmed by the priest who had married them not two hours before!

Viola heard this information with horror no less than that which filled the duke. She stared from Olivia to Orsino, whose look of rage and hurt almost wilted her. That he should think she would betray him thus; that Olivia could believe she would betray him thus … !

Olivia, for her part, looked from Orsino to Viola in panic. Where was the eager lover of two hours ago, the man who had leapt to her love with the heat of passion that matched her own?

While all the while Antonio looked on, scowling at Viola, as did Orsino, as did Olivia, each believing this youth to be a master of betrayal, a man without a soul, heart or honour of any kind …

Into this bewildered circle stumbled Sir Andrew

with bleeding head, followed by Toby Belch, clutching his head and moaning, fleeing (so they said) from the duke's young gentleman, Cesario, who had viciously set upon them but a moment ago ...

And there he stood! Even Sir Toby now shrank a little from the sight of him ...

Everyone stared at Viola. A liar, a betrayer, and now a breaker of men's heads!

And a man who could by magic split himself in two! For suddenly a second Cesario sprang before their astounded eyes. 'I am sorry, madam, I have hurt your kinsman,' he cried out to Lady Olivia. 'Pardon me, sweet one, even for the vows we made each other, so little time ago!'

There was a silence. Olivia stared from the Cesario who now acknowledged his vows to her to the Cesario who denied them. Viola gazed with fast-beating heart upon this mirror-image of herself and scarcely dared to hope ...

The duke whispered, 'One face, one voice and two persons!' While Sebastian, for the newcomer was he, spotted Antonio and rushed towards him with his hands outstretched, 'Antonio, oh my dear Antonio! How have the hours racked and tortured me since I have lost you!'

'Sebastian, are you he?' said Antonio, suspiciously, for the misery of these past hours had wiped away his trust of any man. 'How have you made division of yourself? An apple, sliced in two, is not more twin than these two creatures! Which is Sebastian?'

For the first time, Sebastian became aware of his other self. He gaped at the apparition: what new madness in this land of madness was this trick? He laughed, for perhaps the trick would laugh itself away. But still it stood there, and still the duke, Olivia, and Antonio stood looking at them both, from one to the other and back again.

'I never had a brother. Nor can I be here and everywhere!' Sebastian assured them, though by now he was beginning to wonder if he could say even this with any certainty. 'But I had a sister … ' and even as he said this, a new hope began to stir in him …

Viola took a step towards him. 'Sebastian was my father; such a Sebastian was my brother, too … ' for in that moment she, at least, had understood …

'Were you a woman,' cried Sebastian, 'I would let my tears fall upon your cheek, and say, "welcome, drowned Viola!"'

With a sweep Viola tore the cap from her head and let her long hair tumble down. 'My father had a mole upon his brow!' she cried.

'And so had mine,' yelled Sebastian.

'And died that day Viola turned thirteen!' Viola shrieked, and fell upon her brother's neck in tears of joy.

And so the tangle was untied, and all explained, forgiven, and repaired. Olivia, who had unwittingly loved a girl and believed herself betrayed, now found herself united, as she longed for, with a man. Viola, whose sorrow for her brother's death had remained with her for three long months, was now miraculously clasped in his living arms. And the duke …

The duke had watched these moments of revelation and discovery with fascination. As the truth began to dawn on him, so was his heart and mind awash with sudden memories of all the months in which his devoted page had offered him companionship, and sympathy … and love …

He turned now to gaze at Viola with an eye and heart uncluttered by his worship of Olivia. He looked at Viola not as a gentle youth to whom he gave his confidence, but as a woman, and in that instant, knew he loved her as he had never loved Olivia. He loved her as a person that he knew and understood and truly cared for, not an idol that he painted in his mind in colours that were not her own …

And he remembered her own words to him. 'Boy,' he said, with a teasing mockery in his eyes, 'you have said to me a thousand times that you never would love any woman as you loved me … '

'And all those sayings will I swear again,' Viola said, throwing all caution to the winds, 'and all those swearings keep as true in soul as is the sun that keeps the day from night … '

'Give me your hand, and let me see you in your woman's clothes,' Orsino cried.

And so two pairs of tangled lovers were untangled,

and retied with the one they loved: Sebastian to Olivia and Orsino to Viola.

But two others languished still alone: Antonio knew that he had lost the companionship of the young man he adored; but yet there was a compensation in the knowledge that no betrayal of his trust had taken place.

And Malvolio? What of Malvolio, poor hood-winked Malvolio, whose fantasy of love had led him to a trap beyond his wildest nightmares?

Followed closely by Malvolio, Feste the jester, true to his word, now delivered a letter from that poor despairing man to Olivia …

And so it came about that Maria's letter, faking Olivia's handwriting was produced. In a moment the plot was laid before Olivia, Malvolio's plight revealed in all its misery, as was the role of Toby, Fabian and Maria and the jester, to say nothing of Sir Andrew Aguecheek … Though these admissions were not given without a full and vivid catalogue of those injuries at Malvolio's hand that had prompted them all to take revenge …

'Alas, how they have baffled you,' sighed Olivia to Malvolio.

'And thus the whirligig of time brings in his revenges,' Feste chanted.

'I'll be revenged on the whole pack of you,' declared Malvolio, his nose returning to its customary height above the ground, his mouth to its customary pinched pout, whirling on his heel with his customary snort, to march away from them.

'He has been notoriously abused,' said Olivia, watching the offended man disappear from sight with sorrow.

'Pursue him,' urged Orsino, for whom no cloud would mar this day of unexpected happiness. 'Entreat him to a peace.' And now he turned with joy towards his faithful page.

'Cesario, come, for so you shall be, while you are a man; but when in other garments you are seen, Orsino's mistress, and his fancy's queen!'

And now the garden of this stately home in fair Illyria was emptied of its lovers gained and lovers lost. Only the jester Feste stayed, to linger in the fading sunshine, and to sing a little, mournful song …

'When that I was and a little tiny boy,

With a hey, ho, the wind and the rain,

A foolish thing was but a toy,

For the rain it raineth every day … '